SPACE RACE

Adapted by Lauren Forte
from the episode "Space Race" written by Greg Johnson
for the series created by Sascha Paladino

Illustrated by Jason Fruchter

 A GOLDEN BOOK • NEW YORK

Miles is excited! He is watching a commercial for the Tomorrowland Space Race on a holo-screen in his family's starship.

"Who will finish first and be awarded this one-of-a-kind *Blast Jet* jet pack? May the best racer win!" said the announcer.

"I hope that's going to be us, Merc!" Miles says to his robo-ostrich. "I really, really, really want to win that jet pack!"

Miles builds a racer.
His mother, father, and
sister come to see it.

"It's finally done," Miles says proudly.
"May I present . . . the **_Photon Flyer_**!"

"What a great design,
Miles!" exclaims his mom.

As the *Stellosphere* zooms to the planet where the race is being held, Miles looks outside and spots his friend's spaceship.

"Miles to Pipp," he says into his QuestCom. "Look out your starboard window."

"Hi!" says Pipp.

"How did your racer come out?" Miles asks.

"It's pretty fast. Hope you can keep up," Pipp teases. "See you at the starting line!"

Meanwhile, Gadfly, the evil alien outlaw, is scheming to enter the race.

"I will win that jet pack!" he shouts to his holo-goons. "And since only children can be in this race, that's what I'll pretend to be!"

He steps into a machine that disguises him as a kid.

Then Gadfly tests the secret sonic blaster he added to his racing ship. The blaster can make the other ships blast off course.

"Those racers won't know what hit them!" he shouts.

"It's race time!"

"Welcome, one and all, to the **_Tomorrowland Space Race_**!" announce Admiral Watson and Admiral Crick. "As the heads of the Tomorrowland Transit Authority, we are happy to introduce today's racers!"

"First we have the Fling Shot, piloted by Blodger Blopp," Admiral Watson says.

"Next up is the Photon Flyer, piloted by Miles Callisto."

"And Merc, his robo-ostrich," adds Admiral Crick.

"Third is the Hot Saucer, piloted by Pipp Whipley."

"And last, it's the RamJammer, piloted by a new kid named Flyspeck Sapien," says Admiral Watson.
"Does that boy need a shave?" Admiral Crick wonders out loud.

Miles' family joins him at the starting line.

"Win or lose, make this a race you can be proud of," his dad tells him.
"I will!" Miles promises.

"Launch in T minus three . . . two . . . one . . . **WHOOSH!**" And the racers zoom off toward the blaster flats.

Blodger takes the lead. But then Gadfly fires his secret sonic blaster at the little green alien.

Blodger's racer spins out and gets hit by a burst of ice from a cryo-geyser. He is out of the competition.

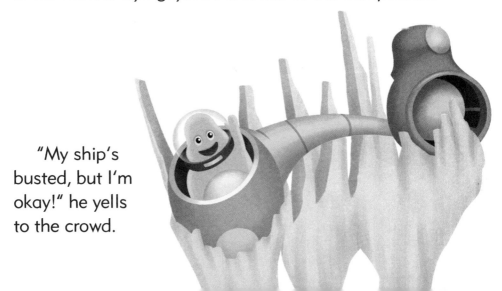

"My ship's busted, but I'm okay!" he yells to the crowd.

"Oh, no!" cries Pipp when he sees Gadfly heading toward Miles. Pipp speeds up and quickly swerves very close to Gadfly's racer, knocking it off course.

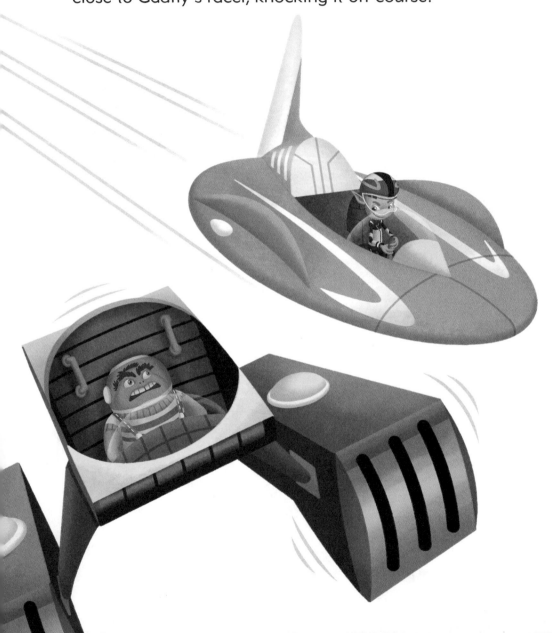

"Miles, that cheater was about to use some kind of energy blast on your racer," Pipp shouts. "Just like he did to Blodger's."

"Thanks for blocking it, Pipp. I owe you!" Miles yells back.

It's a tight race as the three ships soar and weave through the canyons.

Before long, Gadfly pulls alongside Pipp and fires his blaster.

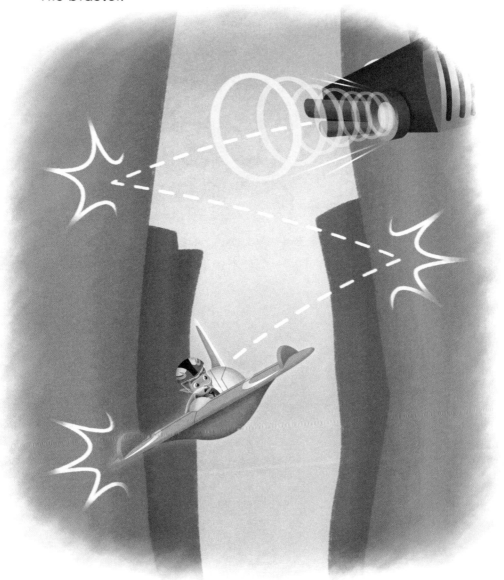

"Aww, wormholes!" Pipp hollers as his ship crashes against the rocks.

Miles turns his Photon Flyer around. "We would've been out of this race if Pipp hadn't helped us," he reminds Merc.

"What are you doing? You could still win this!" Pipp yells to Miles, who is pushing a boulder off the Hot Saucer.

"We started this race together, and we're gonna finish it together," Miles tells him.

"You're a galactic friend," says Pipp, smiling.

"Flyspeck is coming down the final stretch!" the admirals announce.

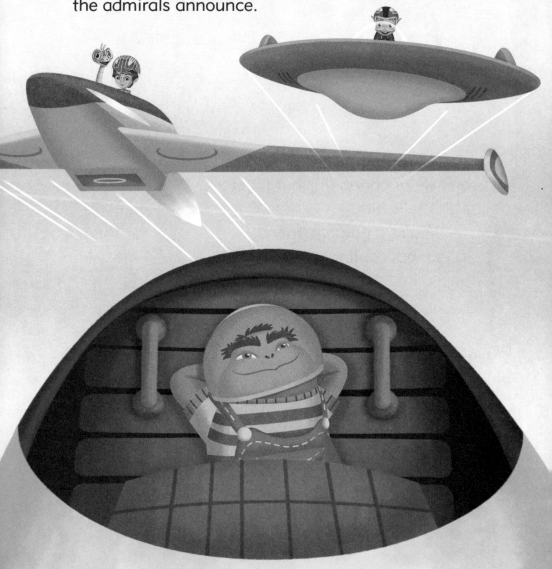

Evil Gadfly is so sure he's going to win, he slows down and relaxes. Pipp and Miles catch up and speed right past him.

"Ready to finish this thing?" asks Miles.
"Oh, yeah!" calls Pipp.

The two racers zoom to the finish line—with Pipp
flying slightly ahead of his friend.

"Hey, Merc, are you sad we didn't win?" Miles asks as they climb out of the Photon Flyer.

"Ehhhh-ahhh," squawks Merc.
Miles grins. "Me neither!"

"AND THE TOMORROWLAND PILOT OF THE FUTURE IS . . . PIPP WHIPLEY! Enjoy your new Blast Jet," Admiral Watson declares.

"I share this victory with my friend Miles Callisto," says Pipp. "I wouldn't be here without him."

"Hey, Miles!" says Pipp.
"Up for another race?"

With a huge smile, Miles
jumps on his Blastboard
and shouts, "You're on!"